Look!Snow!

Other Books by Kathryn O. Galbraith

SOMETHING SUSPICIOUS

WAITING FOR JENNIFER
illustrated by Irene Trivas

ROOMMATES
illustrated by Mark Graham

ROOMMATES AND RACHEL
illustrated by Mark Graham

(Margaret K. McElderry Books)

Margaret K. McElderry Books   Maxwell Macmillan Canada, Inc.
Macmillan Publishing Company   1200 Eglinton Avenue East
866 Third Avenue   Suite 200
New York, NY 10022   Don Mills, Ontario M3C 3N1

Macmillan Publishing Company is part of the Maxwell Communication
Group of Companies.
First edition
Printed in Hong Kong by South China Printing Company (1988) Ltd.
10 9 8 7 6 5 4 3 2 1
The text of this book is set in Lectura Roman.
The illustrations are rendered in colored pencil and oil stick.

Library of Congress Cataloging-in-Publication Data
Galbraith, Kathryn Osebold.
Look! Snow! / by Kathryn O. Galbraith ; illustrated by
Nina Montezinos. — 1st ed.
p.   cm.
Summary: The first snow of the season brings great enjoyment to
the town's human and animal inhabitants.
ISBN 0-689-50551-5
[1. Snow—Fiction.]   I. Montezinos, Nina, ill.   II. Title.
PZ7.G1303Lo   1992
[E]—dc20   91-28250

Look! Snow!

Kathryn O. Galbraith

Illustrated by Nina Montezinos

MARGARET K. McELDERRY BOOKS
New York

Maxwell Macmillan Canada
Toronto

Maxwell Macmillan International
New York   Oxford   Singapore   Sydney

To Matthew Charles and his big sister, Jessica
And once again to Steve
—K.O.G.

For Joe, with Love
—N.M.

"Look! Snow!"

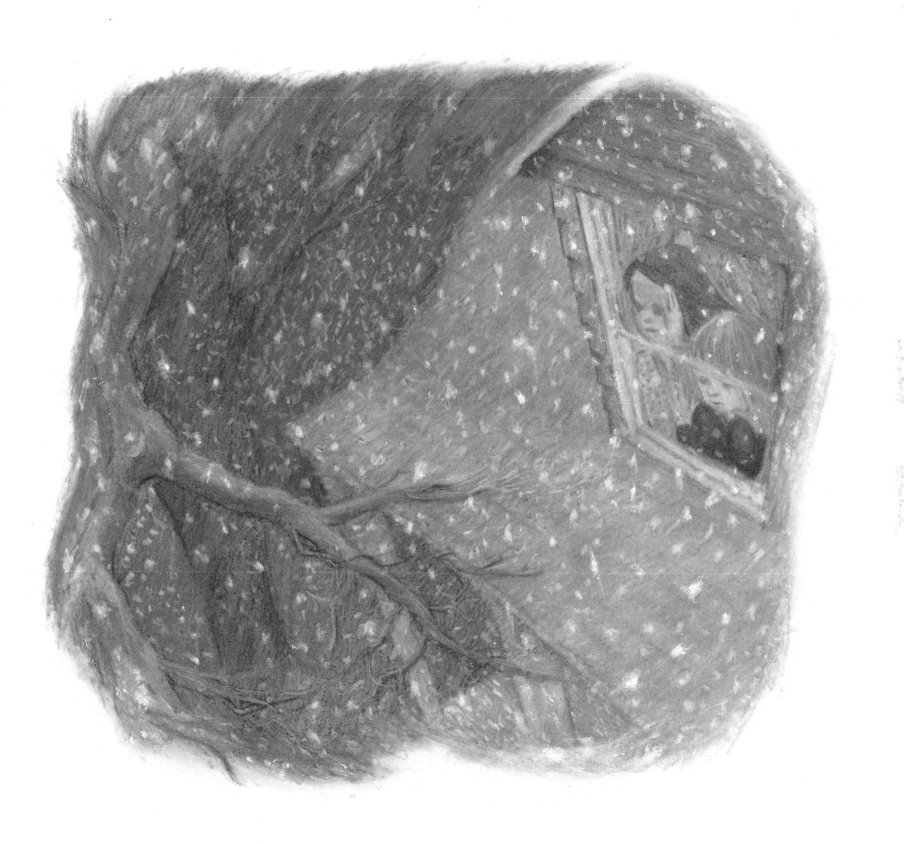

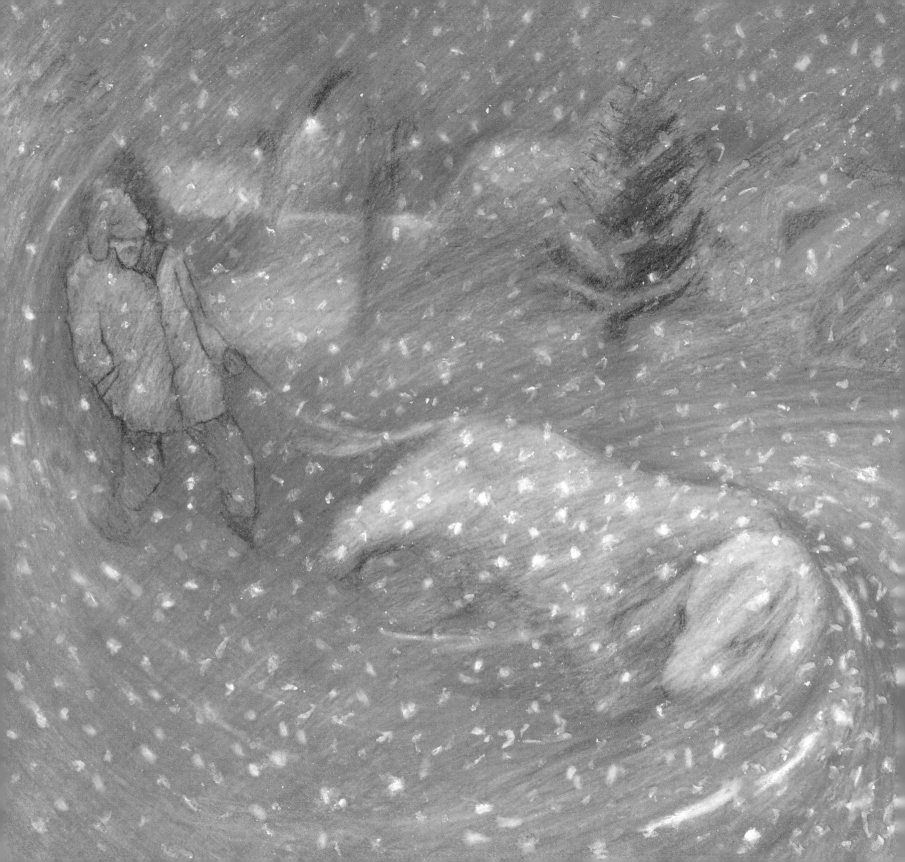

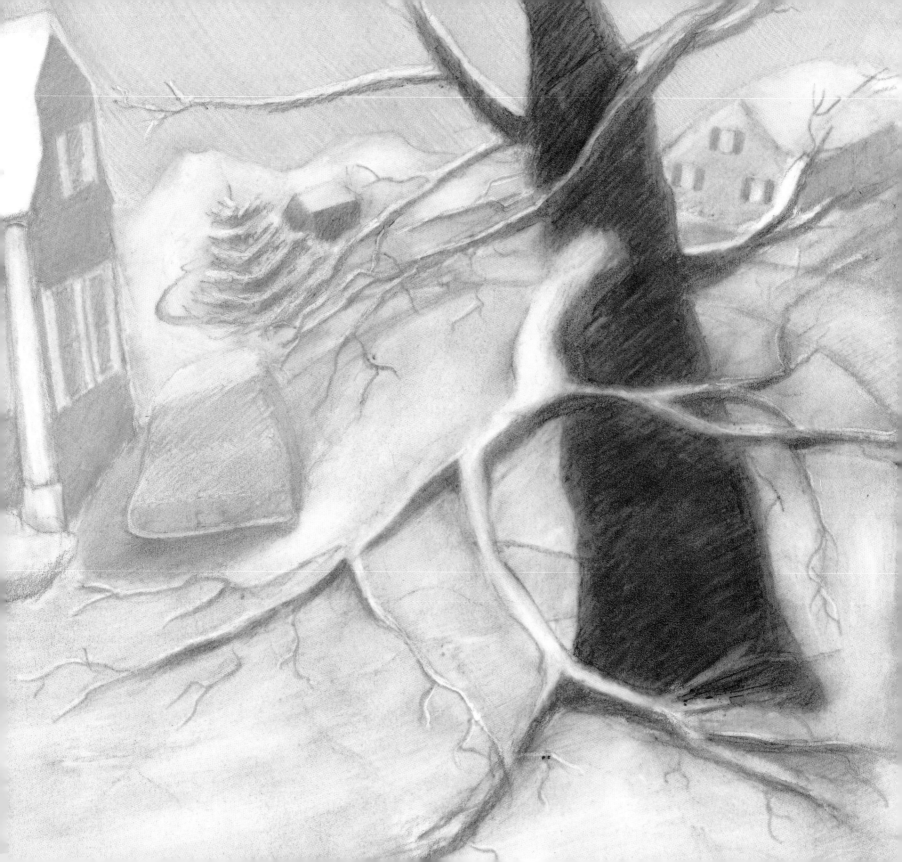

"The following schools are closed for today:

Dayton, Central…"

"...Southcentral,

Pearson,

Hayden..."

"...Foss...Washington..."

"McCormick!
It's a snow day!"

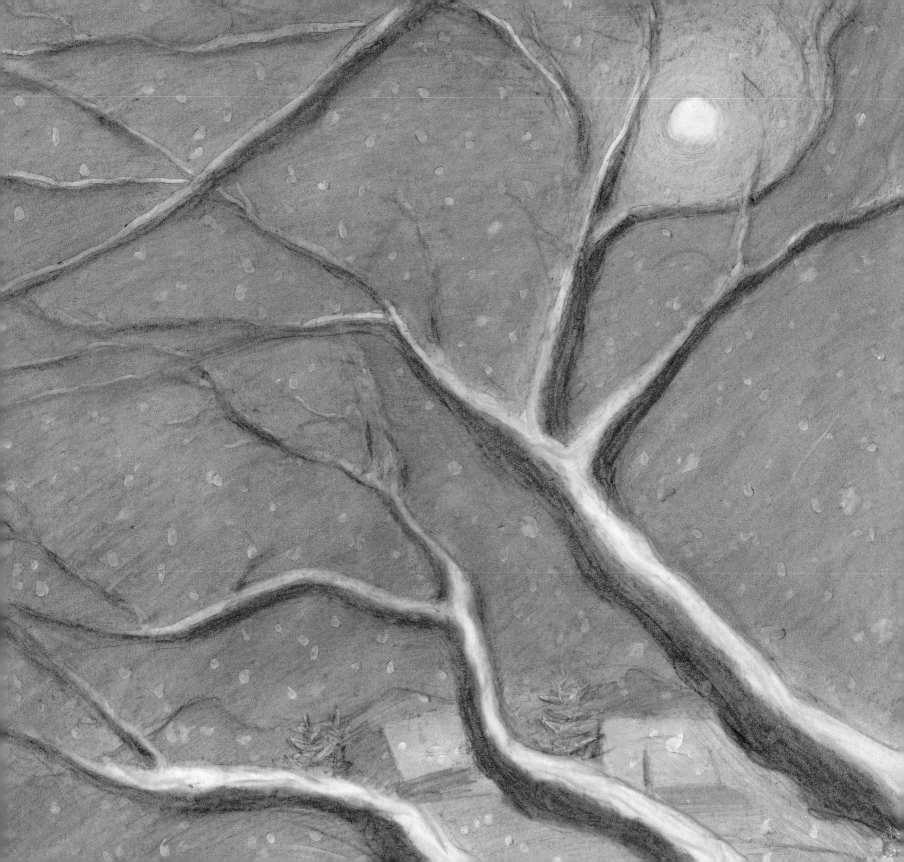

"Look! Snow!"